SPACE AGE

Derek Farr

Illustrated by
Claire Fulford

Published by New Generation Publishing in 2020

Copyright © Derek Farr 2020

First Edition

The author asserts the moral right under the Copyright, Designs and Patents Act 1988 to be identified as the author of this work.

All Rights reserved. No part of this publication may be reproduced, stored in a retrieval system or transmitted, in any form or by any means without the prior consent of the author, nor be otherwise circulated in any form of binding or cover other than that which it is published and without a similar condition being imposed on the subsequent purchaser.

Paperback ISBN: 978-1-80031-702-4
Hardback ISBN: 978-1-80031-701-7
Ebook ISBN: 978-1-80031-700-0

www.newgeneration-publishing.com

New Generation Publishing

Dedicated to:

Annabel, Megan, Tristan, Alex, Ben, Tommy, Kate, Georgia, Great Grandad GRAY and Rosie.

Silly Grandad xxx

Written during the UK Covid-19 lockdown March – July 2020
by Silly Grandad and illustrated by Claire – with help from
Great Grandad GRAY, Rosie Fulford and eight special grandchildren.

Profits to an outstanding Residential Care Home:

Grace Muriel House 'The Abbeyfield St. Albans Society Ltd.'

(Registered Charity No: 211934)

To the amazing staff, volunteers and helpers ALL…

THANK YOU FOR YOUR CARE AND ALWAYS BEING THERE

https://www.abbeyfieldstalbans.co.uk

Our Journey through SPACE...

The MILKY WAY	with ROSIE
BLACK HOLES	with BEN
SOL our SUN	with KATE
MERCURY	with MEGAN
VENUS	with ANNABEL
EARTH	with KATE
The MOON	with GRAY
MARS	with ALEX
JUPITER	with TRISTAN
SATURN	with GEORGIA
URANUS	with TOMMY
NEPTUNE	with GEORGIA
PLUTO	with BEN

Grandad Meerkat needs some help...

I'm Grandad Meerkat, and how do you do; I must just say that I really need YOU.

I'm exploring our SOLAR SYSTEM in the MILKY WAY; the stars and the planets, one every day.

Will you come on a journey up in the sky; find out who might live there and perhaps say hi?

What is their home like, and what do they do; what do they look like, anything like YOU?

Will you help me explore the depths of our SPACE; we'll visit them all with a smile on our face.

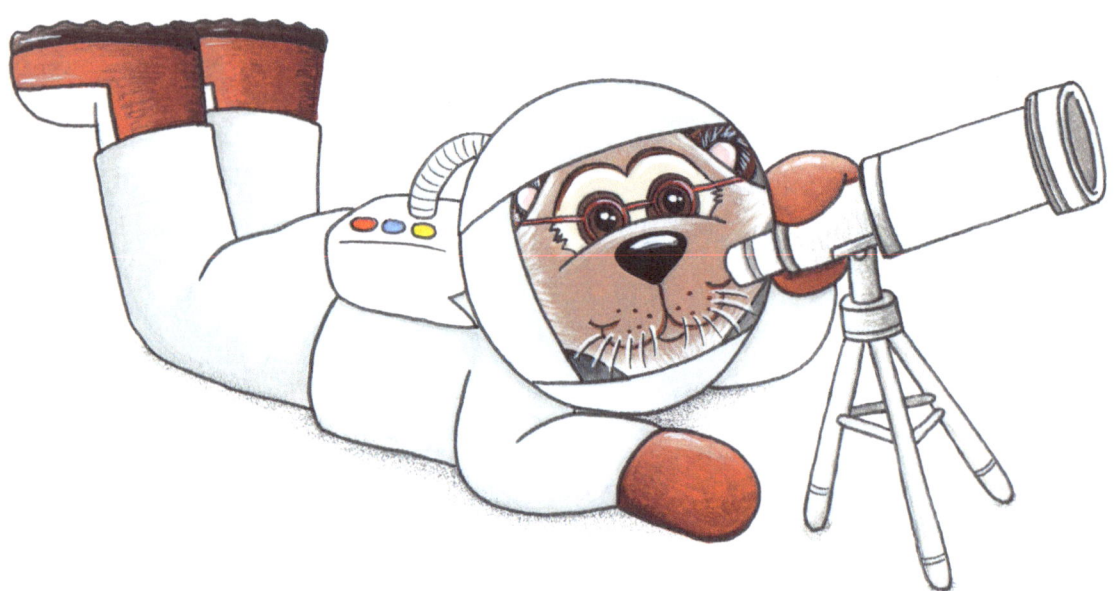

Space Age – The Adventure begins...

Who will come on a journey with me, on our exploration through SPACE;

...Megan, Tristan, Alex, Ben, Tommy, Kate, Georgia and Annabel Grace

- and Great Grandad GRAY and Rosie Fulford too?

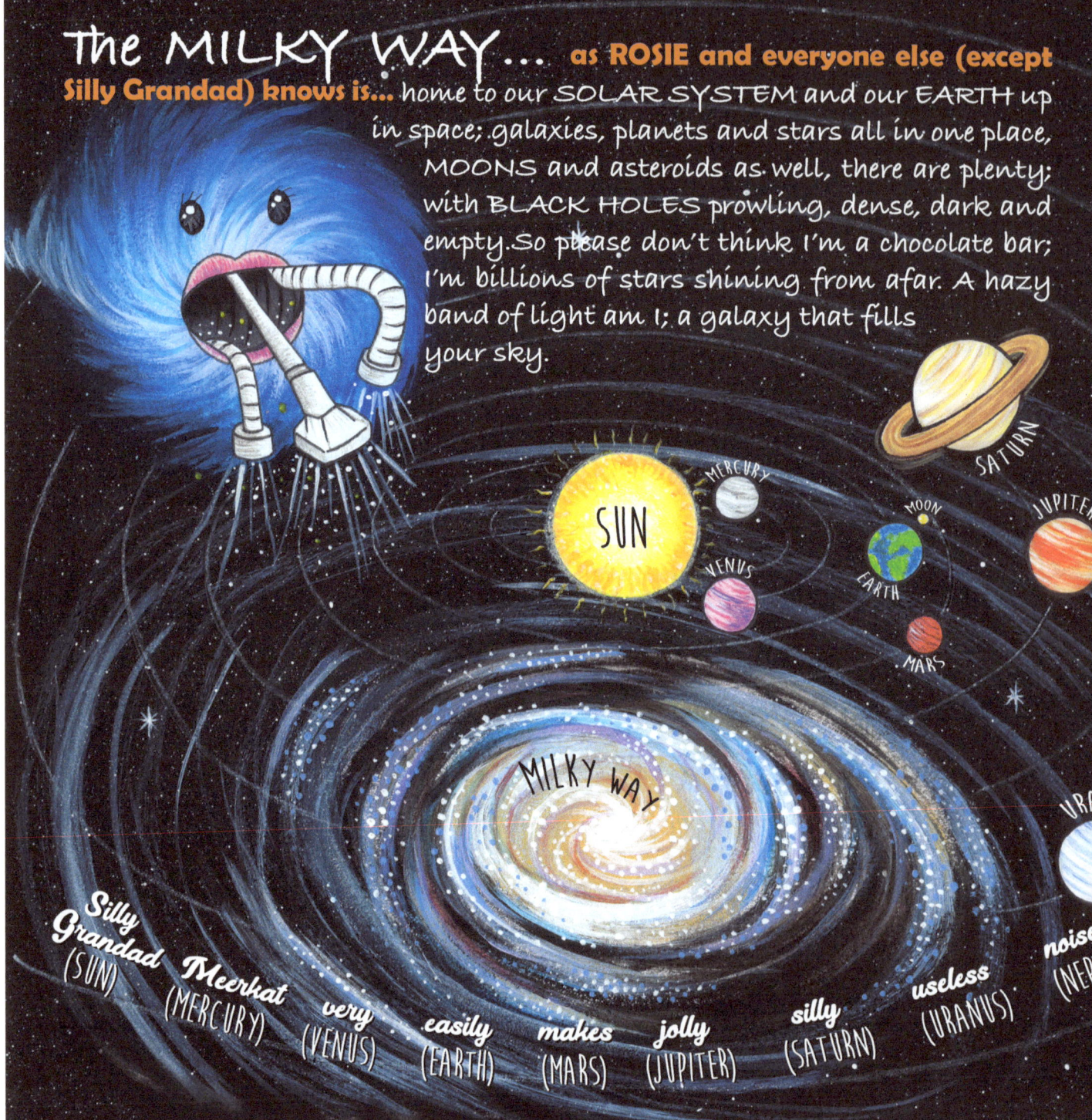

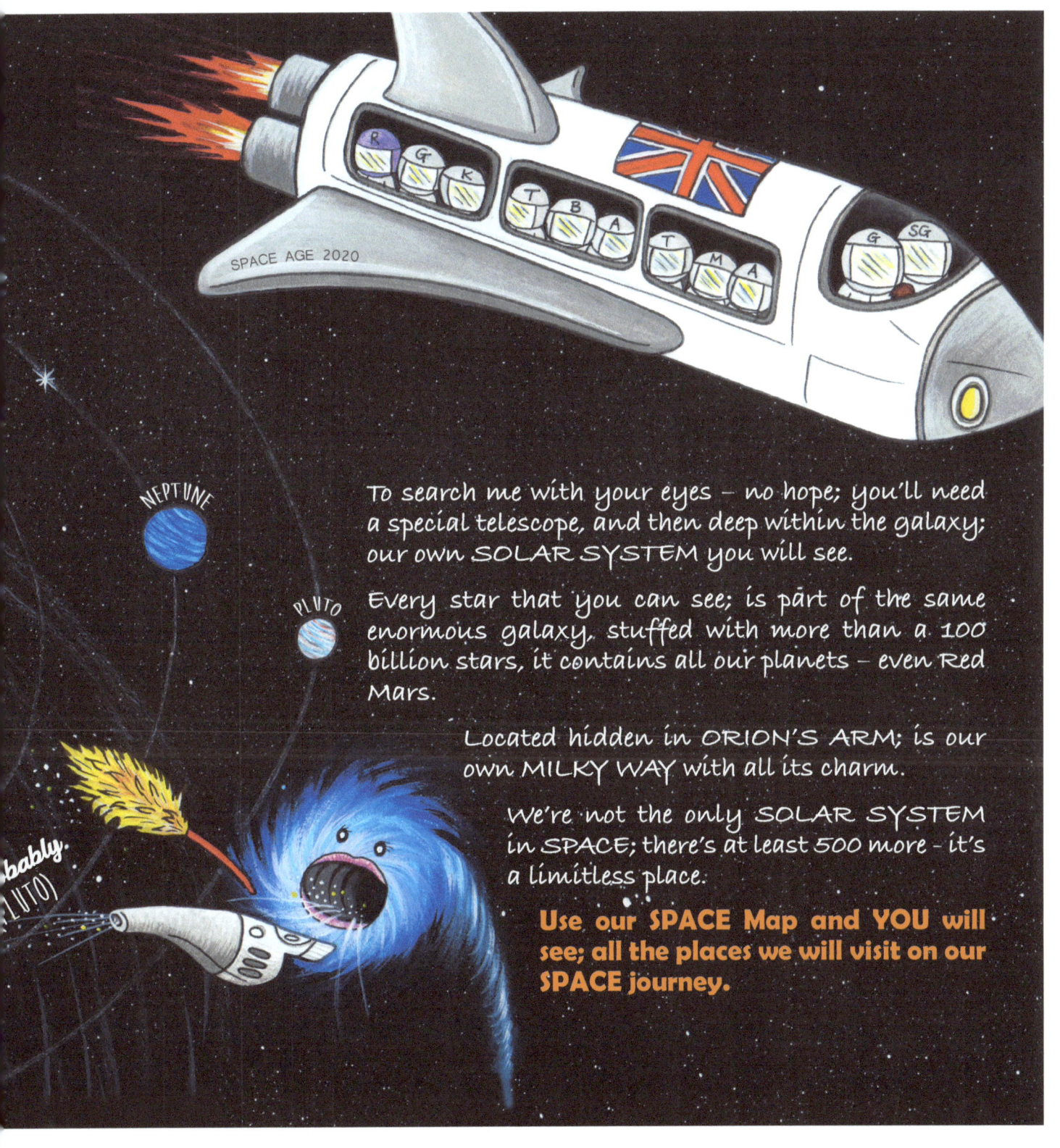

To search me with your eyes – no hope; you'll need a special telescope, and then deep within the galaxy; our own SOLAR SYSTEM you will see.

Every star that you can see; is part of the same enormous galaxy, stuffed with more than a 100 billion stars, it contains all our planets – even Red Mars.

Located hidden in ORION'S ARM; is our own MILKY WAY with all its charm.

We're not the only SOLAR SYSTEM in SPACE; there's at least 500 more – it's a limitless place.

Use our SPACE Map and YOU will see; all the places we will visit on our SPACE journey.

BLACK HOLES... as BEN and everyone else (except Silly Grandad) knows are most odd.

Huge BLACK HOLES, we've found them in our UNIVERSE and wonder what they do; who put them there, who saw them first and are they friendly too?

We don't know where they come from, or what they truly do; I think they must clean up all Outer Space, do YOU?

They must be like giant basking sharks, with enormous open jaws; digesting debris, swallowing comets and sucking stars through straws.

Floating about like giant jawed sucking cleaners of many different types; vacuum cylinders, cordless, cyclones dust-bags and even some uprights.

They store their food in vacuum flasks, filled with star dust and debris aplenty; and never tire of swallowing comets- century after century.

Whilst they seem extremely frightening, I don't really think they are; they're the MILKY WAYS' own dustbin creatures, keeping us all free from harm.

Let's say "thank you basking BLACK HOLES, for all the work you do"; so three loud cheers, and hip-hip hooray from BEN, me and YOU!

What else do YOU think BLACK HOLIANS might do every day; how do they move, where do they go and when do they ever have any time to play?

Can YOU help Silly Grandad as he goes on his way; with KATE next, to SOL our SUN, so let's blast away.

SOL our SUN... as KATE and everyone else (except Silly Grandad) knows is...

the centre of our universe and the biggest star around; hot, gold, and yellow, at least 5 billion years old.

She really is an amazing YELLOW DWARF STAR; having solar winds, eruptions and bellowing heat from afar.

If Yellow Dwarfs do live there, they'd need mountains of sun spray; and extremely fire-proof skins to keep the heat and flames at bay.

We think SOLIANS must be wispy, smoky and very tiny things; - no arms, no legs, just flame gold bodies with large fan-like wings.

Do they breathe fire like dragons, and spout gaseous yellow screams; and need very dark glasses when they play and dream?

How would they speak and what might they say; ... and can we hear them from 93 million miles away?

What do YOU think SOLIANS might do every day; what will they eat, and how would they play?

Can YOU help Silly Grandad as he goes on his way; with MEGAN next, to MERCURY, so let's blast away.

MERCURY... as MEGAN and everyone else (except Silly Grandad) knows is...

the nearest planet to SOL our SUN and next to VENUS in our sky; named after the Roman Messenger God, she likes to say hi.

The smallest of planets, she spins very fast; - a MERCURIAN year is only 88 days from first to last,

She blows hot and cold and is nearest the SUN; but hasn't got a moon, not even one.

Silvery craters, cosy caves, and hollows in wrinkly hills; that's where our MERCURIANS hide from the heat and the chills.

They are the heaven's winged messengers, everyone; sending letters and news to the planets, stars and SUN.

With their silvery wings and maps of the skies; they deliver the news - the truth, and the lies.

No one has ever seen their faces, we only spy wings; as letters and parcels cover their bodies and things.

If you get a message it will surely come; delivered by MERCURIANS from the planets or our SUN.

So please think of them working every single day; whilst you are perhaps fast asleep, or even at play.

What do YOU think MERCURIANS might do every day; what will they eat, and what would they play?

Can YOU help Silly Grandad as he goes on his way; with ANNABEL next, to VENUS, so let's blast away.

VENUS... as ANNABEL and everyone else (except Silly Grandad) knows is...

named, I'm told after the Goddess of Love fame; VENUS is the only planet with a female name.

This bright Morning Star has a year shorter than ours; only 225 days, that's about 5,000 hours.

It is so terribly hot as it's nearer the Sun; and whilst a sister to EARTH, it spins backwards for fun.

VENUSHES folk must live in pink, purply clouds; formed from very hot water boiled into shrouds.

The heat has evaporated all the water to nowt; so that VENUS today, is in permanent drought.

VENUSHES have no moons to spy, in their cloudy sky; so spend time watching EARTH as we spin by.

Blowing kisses in every direction each day; they send love to the planets as they go on their way.

They are happy and loveable just like you; and like chatting and eating and partying too.

Sandwiched neatly between MERCURY and planet EARTH; it's a good place to visit, explore and to search.

If you ever think to go there, then please, make a plan; and remember it's very hot, so do take a fan.

What do YOU think VENUSHES might do every day; what will they eat, and what would they play?

Can YOU help Silly Grandad as he goes on his way with KATE next, to our EARTH, so let's blast away.

EARTH...

Our EARTH, as KATE and everyone else (except Silly Grandad) knows (he is forgetful!) is a wonderful place...

A thousand years ago Old English ERTHA was our name; we re-arranged the letters... it was a good game.

We've a lot of nicknames – 'Blue Planet', 'The World' are just two; but 'Gaia' and 'Terra' are other ones too.

The 3rd planet nearest the Sun, formed 4.5 billion years ago; we've a powerful magnetic field and gravity you well know.

We've only one natural satellite – our bright MOON; ... but I'll tell you much more about that very soon.

We harbour life of many kinds on land, in the sky and the seas; animals, mammals, fish, birds, and of course the bees.

As the 5th largest planet in our Solar System in space; we're just the right size - a really amazing place.

We've things that swim, fly, slither and walk; and even some that twitter, sing, bellow and talk.

Sandwiched between the planets of VENUS and MARS; we're near to the SUN, the MOON and the Stars.

We really are very lucky to be in this place; just make sure you ALL keep a smile on your face.

What do YOU think WE can start to do better; to keep Mother EARTH, in really fine fettle?

Let's all try our best to make the EARTH safe; and to keep it for always, a beautiful place.

Can YOU help Silly Grandad as he goes on his way; with GRAY next, to our MOON, so let's blast away.

The MOON... as GRAY and everyone else (except Silly Grandad) knows is...

EARTH'S very own satellite; and is in our skies every night.

The make-believe MOON, is made out of cheese; and when it is full, the Werewolves will sneeze;

and howl until they've had their fill; I do hope the cheese will make them ill.

When it is at its smallest crest; to bring you luck you'll find it best;

... to swap your money, turn it over; with this and good luck, you'll be in clover.

But none of this of course is true; and here are some facts I give to you...

The sky, I light up in the night; I'm Mother EARTH's own satellite.

A quarter of the size of you; of visitors I've had a few (*12 actually*).

MOONIES have found it quiet up here; because there is no atmosphere;

the gravity is different too; you'll only weigh a sixth of you.

I orbit monthly – take a ride; watch the seas, I move the tide.

I'm always up there, every night; to keep your future strong and bright,

What do YOU think MOONIES might do every day; how do they hear, and what would they play?

Can YOU help Silly Grandad as he goes on his way with ALEX next, to MARS, so let's blast away.

MARS... as ALEX and everyone else (except Silly Grandad) knows is...

A dusty RED terrestrial planet is MARS, to our right; named after the Roman God of War who will fight; anything invading its' territory - day or night.

About half the size of EARTH with our trees; it has the same land mass, but just doesn't have seas.

It's home to Olympus Mons the biggest volcano of all; standing an amazing 21 kilometres tall, we think it's still active with some lava flows; so when YOU visit MARS, watch out for your toes.

MARS has two moons - one named PHOBUS - that's Fear; and the other means Panic - DEIMOS, I hear.

MARTIANS go out in many a cold dusty storm; wear Covid face masks and red cloaks to keep warm.

I think they must be like huge flying ants; but with large blood-shot eyes and tight scarlet pants.

Their year is double the length of our EARTH's hours; they've loads of time to make war... and grow flowers?

Red battlefield poppies or crimson carnations they like best; they grow in most places and are resistant to pest.

They practise their fighting in big boxing rings; which is why they all have strong, collapsible wings.

But I think they're friendly and if they visit EARTH, our place; we should welcome them fondly, with smiles and good grace.

What do YOU think MARTIANS might look like, what do they wear; and are they happy with never a care?

Can YOU help Silly Grandad as he goes on his way with TRISTAN next, to JUPITER, so let's blast away.

JUPITER... as TRISTAN and everyone else (except Silly Grandad) knows is...

The giant of our planets with a hurricane RED SPOT; it is the protector of our galaxy and certainly does a lot.

JUPITER's a great huge magnet, directing harm far away; this King of Gods stops asteroids and comets colliding each day.

11 times larger than EARTH... our very own home; JUPITER is hot, red and yellow, a huge great dome.

It is 5 Billion years since JUPITER's birth; he's a little bit older than our planet EARTH.

I'm told that if you visit there, diamonds you'll find; as they rain from the skies - I'm sure you won't mind!

You'll find him next to SATURN and also by MARS; with lots of moons and many rings he's the King of all Stars.

It's the fastest spinning planet - 12 years to orbit the SUN; so JUPITERIANS get giddy and that's really not fun.

JUPITERIAN's move at an amazing speed for their size; with jet propelled feet and big muscled thighs.

I think they are tall with huge biceps and great claws; catching rocks, zapping rays when they're playing outdoors.

I think we should thank them for all that they do; come on everybody 3 cheers for JUPITER - no no, do not boo!

What do YOU think JUPITERIANS might do every day; how do they exercise, and what do they play?

Can YOU help Silly Grandad as he goes on his way with GEORGIA next, to SATURN, so let's blast away.

SATURN…   as GEORGIA and everyone else (except Silly Grandad) knows is…

the prettiest of all the planetary things; with seven rainbow bright, spinning gas rings.

A giant of our planets and the oldest of all; it's a tilted, spinning, yellow gaseous ball.

It's NINE times larger than our EARTH I am told; has 80 plus Moons and is really somewhat cold.

Its' Moon TITAN, is huge with its own atmosphere; it's larger than MERCURY - that's perfectly clear.

Sandwiched betwixt JUPITER and URANUS, the God of the Sky; it's a good place to visit, explore and say hi.

SATURNICORNS are the most pleasant of beasts; they are joyful, fun unicorns, the best you could meet.

They slide round their rings smiling with glee; in their playground high up in our Galaxy.

They speak in gas bubbles of different hue; but I don't really understand them, what about you?

10 hours is the length of one SATURN day; so not much time to sleep, drink or play,

but it takes longer to go around SOL our SUN; … 29 years is plenty of time for games and fun.

I don't know if you knew that our own Saturday; was named after SATURN, in a Roman way?

What do YOU think SATURNICORNS might do every day; what treats do they eat, and tricks do they play?

Can YOU help Silly Grandad as he goes on his way; with TOMMY next, to URANUS, so let's blast away.

URANUS... as TOMMY and everyone else (except Silly Grandad) knows is...

named the King of the Skies and is the only Greek God; a grandfather to JUPITER and SATURN's old dad.

It's an ice giant planet coloured all methane-blue; with a rock and iron core, it's the coldest planet too.

FOUR times the size of our EARTH where we live; it has 27 moons and is certainly big.

The moons are named after Shakespearian folk; - Ariel, Oberon, Titania and others – for a joke?

That it has 13 bright and dark rings is certainly true; and rotates on its side and goes backwards too.

It turns on its axis in 17 hours and a bit; but to go round the SUN is an 84-year trip.

URANIAN's are giant diamond miners, all ghostly, greeny-blue; with big smiley faces and bodies to see through.

They collect mountains of jewels, in large spade like hands; and wear huge sparkly ribbons and iron head bands.

URANIANS tell stories and perform lots of plays; their Shakespearian theatre is open all days.

They speak in bellows, puffing out signals of cloud; and it gets very confusing when there is a crowd.

Dressing-up in odd costumes whenever they can; they quote lines from the plays - actors to a man.

Which plays do YOU think URANIANS might perform every day; and how do they dress, eat, sing, dance and play?

Can YOU help Silly Grandad as he goes on his way; with GEORGIA next, to NEPTUNE, so let's blast away.

NEPTUNE... as GEORGIA and everyone else (except Silly Grandad) knows is...

named after the God of the Sea; and is the farthest planet from YOU and ME.

It's FOUR times larger than EARTH where we are; has many moons and is a very cold star.

I think like our sea, it is icy and blue; and if anyone lives there, they are not like YOU.

NEP-TUNIANS all live in dark icy seas; - they're huge, shiny blue dragons who so like to please.

Having trident shaped flippers, sharp pointed backs; you really would not expect them to relax...

they like to make music and bellow-out tunes; whilst singing to each of their 14 bright moons.

They certainly must live extremely long lives; since an orbit for Neptune takes a very long time-

165 years to spin just one time around; gives them loads of time to make music and sound.

Despite their sharp teeth and frightening form; they are friendly to visitors and their welcome is warm,

if you go for a visit on a simple day trip; it is best that you space-walk from your rocket ship.

What do YOU think NEP-TUNIANS might do every day; what do they eat, and what would they play?

Can YOU help Silly Grandad as he goes on his way with BEN next, to PLUTO, so let's blast away.

PLUTO… as BEN and everyone else (except Silly Grandad) knows was…

named 90 years ago by a girl just eleven; after the God of the Underworld… but it's found up in heaven?

It first was a full planet, then not it was felt; and now is a 'Dwarf Planet' in the Kuiper Belt.

Smaller than our MOON, it is not very big; but I doubt that any PLUTONIANS would give a fig.

It orbits our SUN nearly 4 billion miles away; and 150 EARTH hours make one PLUTO day.

It has 5 moons that orbit, the largest of which; is Charon - named after the mythical River Styx;

…a place where the ferrymen took Roman souls; please don't talk of that, it reminds me of ghouls.

PLUTO has amazing bright blue skies; and a huge heart-shaped glacier, and that's not lies.

It snows all the time, and would land on your head; but the snow isn't white, it's actually dark red.

Like humanoid cats with white fluffy fur and big ginger spots; PLUTONIANS have long spikey tails covered in dots.

They need to use snow-boards or wear skis when they go; because its amazingly icy and covered in snow.

I think all these creatures are incredibly friendly; and they meet up each day for, their morning assembly.

They like to spend time having red snow-ball fights; and will play in the snow wearing head band torch lights.

What do YOU think PLUTONIANS might do every-day, what will they eat, and what would they play?

YOU have ALL helped Silly Grandad on our journey through SPACE; let's return now to EARTH, a wonderful place.

Space Age – The Adventure ends...

Silly Grandad with Annabel, Megan, Tristan, Alex and Ben;
...Tommy, Kate, Georgia, plus Rosie and GRAY are home once again.

... to write up their adventures, their discoveries too;
and to wonder if it was all really true?

Lightning Source UK Ltd.
Milton Keynes UK
UKHW051440041220
374595UK00002B/41